LI LUN, Lad of Courage

Books in the Newbery Honor Roll Series

The · Newbery · Honor · Roll

LI LUN
Lad of Courage

Carolyn Treffinger

Illustrations by Kurt Wiese

Walker & Company
New York

This paperback edition published in the United States of America in 1995 by Walker
Publishing Company, Inc.

Published simultaneously in Canada by Thomas Allen & Son Canada,
Limited, Markham, Ontario

Library of Congress Cataloging-in-Publication Data
Treffinger, Carolyn.
Li Lun, lad of courage / Carolyn Treffinger : illustrations by
Kurt Wiese.
p.   cm. — (The Newbery honor roll)
Originally published: Nashville : Abingdon-Cokesbury Press, 1947.
Summary: Because of his fear of the sea, a young Chinese boy is
sent to a distant mountain where he proves his bravery.
ISBN 0-8027-7468-7
[1. Courage—Fiction. 2. China—Fiction.] I. Wiese, Kurt,
1887–1974, ill. II. Title. III. Series.
PZ7.T69Li   1995
[Fic]—dc20   95-11285
CIP   AC

Printed in the United States of America

11 12 13 14 15 16 17 18 19 20

Dedicated in Loving Memory
to My Mother and Father

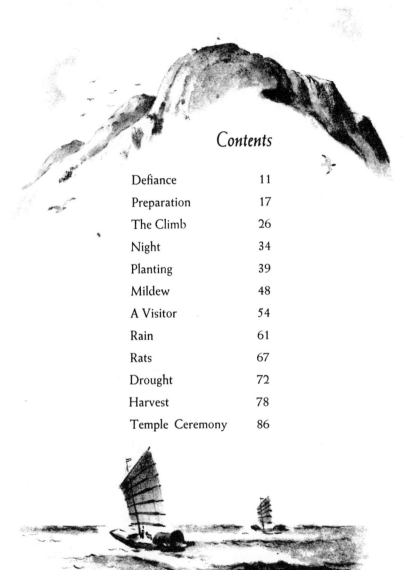

Contents

LI LUN, Lad of Courage

Preparing for the fishing voyage

DEFIANCE

Li Lun crouched behind a huge banyan stump. Cautiously he peered out to watch his father and the other fishermen drag great bags of rice, dried shrimp, and seaweed across the beach and load them onto the sampans. The fishing boats were tied by long ropes which stretched across the sand to the very banyan stump where Li Lun was hiding.

Back and forth went the men from beach to boat, boat to beach, every man with a bag on his back. Groups of boys with ropes and nets atop their heads swashed through the water, singing and shouting.

"I won't go with them," Li Lun told himself firmly. "I won't! I won't!" He thumped his fists against the stump.

Well he knew that soon his father would call his name. For today the men were taking with them their sons — every boy who was ten years of age. This would be the boys' man-making trip; their first fishing voyage.

On this island off the coast of China everyone fished for a living. Fish, shrimp, and seaweed for their eating they could get themselves. But rice they must bring from the mainland many miles away across the rough channel.

On a clear day the fisherfolk of Blue Shark Island could see the mountains along the China coast. And the people on the mainland could see Lao Shan, the highest mountain on Blue Shark Island, and sometimes, at its side and a little behind, Lo Shan, where the North Temple was built.

The men were loosening the ropes which held the sampans.

"I won't go! I won't go!" repeated Li Lun and he clenched his fingers in the sand. He hoped that Teng Lun, his father, might forget about him. But he knew that would not be. Oh, if only he were not so afraid of sea water!

Li Lun's dark eyes searched the distant waters fearfully. Evil spirits swam under those deep rolling waters. Li Lun knew that sometimes one of them rose out of the depths, riding on a big blue wave to snatch a poor fisherman out of a sampan so quickly that he could not even cry out.

Li Lun pushed back his straight black hair and crouched closer to the sand. He looked down at his new blue shirt. If only it were gray, like the stump! Or brown, like his trousers. Maybe then his father would not see him.

On the shore sat the women, watching the little children who played about them, and embroidering pretty things for the city shops. The boys and girls who were old enough, had gone to carry sea water to the holes in the rocks on the mountainside. There the sun would evaporate the water and leave the salt. This the children did every day while the fathers and older boys were away fishing. Or, when quiet-water time was past and the men could not fish, while they were busy on the beach drying and salting the fish, making new nets, or repairing old ones. Everyone on Blue Shark Island had to work. Li Lun knew that. Only the littlest children, so tiny they could scarcely walk, were allowed to play.

Li Lun watched the boys, their carrying tasks finished, climb into the sampans. He dug his fingers and toes into the sand and pretended not to hear their shouts.

"Full tide!" cried one of the fishermen.

Slyly Li Lun glanced along the shore. Already some of the men and boys were hoisting yellow sails and red sails into the breeze. The wind caught hold of the sails and pulled them seaward. The boats looked like huge bats skimming close above the water.

Li Lun held his breath. Perhaps his father would think he had climbed into another boat and was already on his way to sea. Breathlessly he waited for the wind to fill all the sails and pull the boats out into the deep water.

"Li Lun!" called Teng Lun. "Come!"

"I won't go," Li Lun reminded himself, even as his feet took him obediently toward the boat.

Motionless he stood beside his father, his eyes fixed on the huge eye painted on the side of the sampan. The eye that showed the fishing boat the way to travel in deep waters.

"Climb in!" commanded his father as the men picked up the oars.

Li Lun did not move, except to dig his toes deeper into the sand. "I am not going, Father," he announced in a small voice.

"What is that you say?" asked Teng Lun in amazement. "Climb in at once!"

"No, most honorable father," said Li Lun again. "I cannot go!"

"And why can you not go?" asked Teng Lun sarcastically. "Is it that my son is afraid of sea water?"

Li Lun did not raise his eyes. He bit his lips and a red flush covered his face. Each of his fists was a tight ball. Slowly he nodded assent.

"A son of Teng Lun afraid of sea water!" repeated his father, in astonishment. "A son of Teng Lun a coward!"

Li Lun raised his eyes and looked at his father pleadingly.

"I will pull seaweed from the shore," he promised. "I will mend fishing nets. I will do anything, most honorable father. Only, I beg you, let me stay on the land." His voice was tight

14

and harsh from fear. He turned his head to hide trembling lips.

Titters of amusement came from the nearest sampan. The fishermen in near-by boats began to sneer contemptuously at Teng Lun and his son.

Their shouts of derision made the usually calm man lose his temper. Angrily he slapped the flat of his palm against his son's face. "I will have no son of mine a coward!" he screamed.

At sight of the disturbance Li Lun's mother came running up, her baby on her back. She looked at Li Lun's shaking figure, still firm in its determination not to get into the boat. But she could only stand helplessly beside her son.

"Afraid of sea water!" jeered the boys from the sampans. "Afraid of sea water!"

"Most honorable husband—" Wang Lun spoke tremblingly as she pulled her brown, knee-length jacket tighter about her—"I have feared this day. I have known that our son liked not the sea. But remember, Li Lun's most honorable grandfather never went out on the sea. He was ever a lover of the soil. The boy is not to blame if he loves the land and fears the sea. Give him, I pray, some tasks on the land instead."

The boys in the fishing boats were silent now, wondering what would happen.

Teng Lun looked at his wife and hesitated. Then he exclaimed angrily, "Very well! I will give him a land task that will make him beg for the sea!"

He reached into the deep inner pocket of his brown fishing jacket and took something from it.

"Open your hands!" commanded Teng Lun. Into Li Lun's palms he counted seven grains of rice, still in the husks. "Take this rice to the top of Lao Shan!" shouted Teng Lun. "Plant it!"

At the angry tones Li Lun's baby sister began to cry.

"*Sh-h-h!*" quieted the mother.

So angry was Teng Lun that his breath came in gasps. "And do not come back until you have grown seven times as many grains as I have given you. . . . You will be far enough from sea water on Lao Shan!" he scoffed.

Turning quickly, he splashed to the side of the sampan, climbed in, and grasped one of the heavy oars.

"Come along," Wang Lun urged Li Lun gently.

With downcast head Li Lun followed his mother to their tiny home. His heart was heavy with the jeers which reached them from the face of the deep green sea water. He covered the sting of his cheek with his hand. Yet in spite of all this there was a lightness in his heart, because his feet were still on solid earth.

Suddenly he stopped and looked long at that highest mountain which he must climb—Lao Shan, the Sorrow Mountain.

PREPARATION

Li Lun looked lovingly around the one room of the little house in the Village of Three Firs where he lived with his parents, his three younger brothers and baby sister, two cats and three ducks. Already his mother was packing food and clothing. As she worked she talked to Li Lun to ease his mind.

"You will take these two gourd dippers to carry water," she told him. "And those two bamboo poles there in the corner. You may need them."

Li Lun stood looking helplessly at the seven rice grains in his fist. "How does one grow rice?" he asked at length in a small, hopeless voice.

His mother thought for a long moment. Then she answered slowly, "Sun Ling would know. You must learn from Sun Ling how one grows rice."

Carefully Li Lun put the rice grains into the deep pocket

of his brown padded jacket which hung from a peg on the wall. Then he took the coat and went to find the wise old man who lived alone in a shack where Sorrow Mountain touched the sea.

Li Lun thought the old man must have lived forever. No one knew how old Sun Ling was. But everyone knew that he was very wise.

The Old One was sunning himself on the sand when Li Lun found him. Li Lun bowed deeply, then sat on the sand as the old man motioned him to do.

"How does one grow rice, honorable father?" he asked, after he had waited in silence for a full moment.

There was no answer at first. Then, slowly, "Who wants to grow rice?" the Old One wanted to know.

"I want to grow rice," Li Lun announced gravely. "My father has said that I must raise these seven grains." He put his hand into his pocket and held out the rice for Sun Ling to see. "What shall I do?"

"You had best get them in the ground at once," the old man counselled. "One hundred and twenty days for growing rice. Four moon changes."

Li Lun clung to every word which the Old One uttered. Sun Ling talked on and on until the boy thought the rice almost could grow as the old man talked. But Li Lun listened thoughtfully to every sentence and stored it in his mind.

With slow steps the Old One led the boy behind his shack.

Li Lun consults the Old One

"There is some garden soil here," Sun Ling said. "You may have it. I am too weak to plant seeds." He sighed and continued, "My work here is finished. Soon I go to my fathers. When I leave, this shack will be shoved into the deep waters."

The Old One brought a mat from the corner of his hut. Together he and Li Lun scraped the soil from the face of the rock and rolled it into the mat.

"There is little enough ground, but sufficient to grow seven grains of rice. Where will you plant it?"

"My father says I must grow it on top of Lao Shan."

"Ah!" exclaimed Sun Ling with a wise smile. "You will not fish!"

Li Lun hung his head and shuffled away a pace or two.

"I have more to tell you," said the old man kindly.

Li Lun followed Sun Ling to the bench beneath the camphorwood tree. When the Old One had seated himself there, Li Lun squatted on a rock beside him.

"There are other things than fishing," the old man declared. He nodded his head encouragingly and Li Lun noticed that his hair shone like burnished cloud linings. Li Lun's glance rose from the Old One's hair upward to the clouds. "Sun Ling reaches to the very heavens!" he thought.

"Your rice will grow on Lao Shan."

"Thank you, most honorable father. I am glad it is so."

"You will be lonely," Sun Ling went on. "But know you

that your name, Li, means Inner Spirit? That will keep you strong."

Li Lun rose and bowed in deep gratitude.

"Come to see me if I am still here when you return. You may go now."

"Thank you, most honorable father."

Li Lun bowed low. Then, holding the mat tightly, he raced home to his mother.

"Sun Ling knows everything!" he told her. "He helped me get the soil for the plantings. He told me everything that is to be done. I hope—" Li Lun spoke anxiously—"I hope there is water enough up there to flood the plants."

"You have learned much wisdom from Sun Ling," remarked Wang Lun.

"My name, it is Inner Spirit. It will keep me strong."

"I know it is so, my son." Wang Lun turned toward the door. "I will get something for you to eat before you go. Wait here."

Li Lun placed the mat of soil on the earth floor. Then he got the carrying pole and tied the mat in its center. The heaviest load would be on his back. He was still busy arranging and tying the bundles to the pole when his mother returned.

She set a bowl of shrimp and rice on the low table. "Come, Li Lun. Eat against your climb up the mountain."

Li Lun drew his small bench up to the table.

His mother placed an egg beside his plate.

"We have eggs only to celebrate," said Li Lun as he gazed at the prized delicacy.

"Sun Ling has given us reason to celebrate," smiled Wang Lun. "He has made it possible for you to succeed."

Li Lun thought of the long climb ahead of him and ate heartily. He broke the egg. It was like black coffee jelly. Years ago his mother had buried it in sand, thinking to bring it out on some great occasion, possibly his wedding day. Now he was eating it to celebrate for Sun Ling. He was almost happy.

Li Lun did not tell his mother all that Sun Ling had told him. That was for him and Sun Ling only.

As he ate, his mother continued with her embroidery. When he had finished, she handed him two bundles — a large one filled with rice for eating and a smaller one in which was clothing.

Li Lun tied the bundles to his carrying pole. The two gourd dippers he hung around his neck. The bamboo poles he wrapped inside the bedding roll to carry on his back with the soil.

On the end of one of the poles his mother tied a piece of red paper. "For good luck," she said. She did not smile, but her eyes were warm with understanding.

At last Li Lun was ready to leave. He took his baby sister in his arms, rubbed his cheek to hers, then put her gently down. His lips were trembling.

Li Lun's mother brought him food

"In this," said Wang Lun, "are some ground-up dragon bones." She handed him a small tightly wrapped package. "You know when we take dragon bones?"

"Yes, most beautiful mother," Li Lun replied without hesitation. "When there is fear in the heart."

Wang Lun nodded. "But you will fear nothing, Li Lun. Days will be long and nights will be longer. But remember, my son, you will fear nothing."

Li Lun put the package carefully into his big deep pocket with the precious rice grains.

The yellow cat with the big yellow eyes rubbed her soft body against Li Lun's legs and said *meow*. The black cat with the green eyes waved her tail at him from the bench and cried *meo-w-w*.

Li Lun caught up the yellow cat and looked at his mother. "Perhaps I could take the cat with me!" His eyes beamed at the hope of company.

His mother said nothing. She looked at her lap, examining her embroidery for flaws.

The ducks waddled about Li Lun's feet asking for titbits. Li Lun dropped the cat and picked up his favorite white duck. He rubbed his face against her feathers.

"I will take the duck, most beautiful mother. The duck will be company for me."

He glanced at the waiting bundles. "There would not be

food enough for a duck or a cat!" he exclaimed suddenly. He stroked the duck gently and put her down.

"There will be times when your rice grains will mildew." His mother spoke anxiously. "Do you know what to do then?"

"I know, gracious mother. Sun Ling has told me."

Li Lun put over his shoulder the carrying pole with the bundles attached. He raised his eyes toward the mountain.

"Thank you, precious mother." He picked up his woven palmetto hat and went out the door without glancing back to say good-by. His mother must not know that his eyes were filled with tears.

When he had gone a short distance, Li Lun looked around. Wang Lun and his baby sister had already returned to the shore. There with the other women she sat embroidering and watching the small children at play.

Li Lun's heart ached. He wished she would look up. Just once would be enough. But she did not look up. Was it because of sorrow in her heart? Li Lun wondered. Or was she ashamed of him before the other women? Perhaps, he reflected, mothers, like fathers, were unhappy about coward sons.

With sinking heart Li Lun turned and set himself to climbing Lao Shan.

THE CLIMB

It was the hour of short shadows. Li Lun trudged steadily upward over an unbroken trail across what was once melted rock or lava. Like other village children he had often climbed half the height of Lao Shan to gather salt from the rock holes. Li Lun was grateful that the children who were gathering salt today were at home now, having their noonday meal. He would not have to hear their taunts. In an hour he would be out of their sight. He must hurry if he were going to reach the mountaintop before dark.

Sharp-edged stones cut his feet. Setting down his load he slipped into his straw sandals.

Up he climbed, past the place of the rock holes used by the villagers to catch rain water for their tea. Along the shelf-like lava rocks he climbed ever higher and higher.

Perspiration trickled across his forehead and into his eyes.

He set down the bundles to wipe away the moisture and to rest.

Ships and sampans were coming and going on the sea. But not his father's sampan. It was far away by this time.

If only his father had understood why he could not go to sea! Li Lun felt sad in his heart that he had disappointed his father. But he shuddered at the thought of deep waters climbing into the sampans.

He stood up and shouldered the bundles again, happy that he was toiling up the mountain instead of sailing over the sea. The rocks were at peace among themselves; the waves were not.

Li Lun struggled upward until the bundles on his small back seemed like another mountain pushing him down. He balanced the pole on a rock and crawled from under it to rest. With his gourd cup he dipped water from a rock hole to quench his thirst.

While he rested, Li Lun looked in the huge pocket of his jacket to see that the rice kernels were still there. He must not lose them. And the dragon bones. He was relieved to find them both safe.

When he took up his load again, Li Lun wondered about the bamboo poles. They were so clumsy to carry that he was tempted to leave them behind. But his mother had said that he might need them, so he picked them up.

Lizards scurried across the trail to get out of his way. Gray rats poked their heads from behind brown rocks. They were so like the stones that Li Lun would not have seen them except for their curious beady eyes.

Might the rats be evil spirits following him up the mountain? Li Lun wondered. He poked a bamboo pole at one of the places where he saw a rat. "I will have to let them know that I do not want them," he told himself. "The bamboo poles are good for this!"

Up and up Li Lun clambered and rested, clambered and rested. While he relaxed, his eyes followed the gulls skimming over the water and back to shore. Swiftlets flying in and out of the rock holes along the mountain walls attracted his attention. They were building nests and caring for their families. He knew these were the little birds that built the lovely pink-and-white nests which the city shopkeepers collected for bird-nest soup. Li Lun smiled. He would hunt some of the nests and dry them. If he did not eat them, he could sell them later to the shops. There would be plently of time.

He shouldered his burdens and continued the ascent. The sun shone hot upon the lava over which he trod. There was no well-defined path. Here and there grasses and hardy weeds had dared to grow in the cracks which scarred the rocky surface. A few bushes and even trees had gained a foothold.

By now his sandals were worn so smooth that Li Lun slipped frequently. Then he came to a spot where he must either climb up over a rocky ledge or crawl more than his length along the height of a cliff. This he must do by hanging fast to scrubby bush growths.

Li Lun set down his bundles for breathing time. At the west the sun shone upon the water just a mountaintop above it. He must not rest too long.

As he gazed at the sea, Li Lun wondered again about the fishermen. Where were they? He looked at the ledge and at the cliff. At least there was not an evil spirit sitting atop a wave and waiting to crash down upon his head! The thought so encouraged him that he got up, eager to go on. He stretched his arms upward. The ledge, he found, was too high for him to lift his bundles onto it. He must span the cliff. It overlooked the water and sloped upward at a dizzy angle.

Li Lun decided to try the climb first without his bundles. He took hold of some scrubby growths and pulled. They held firmly. He went on, testing each bush before he trusted his weight to it. At last he stood, trembling, on firm rock.

Li Lun burst into a shout of exultation. He was across! The sea was below, but it had not got him! Looking ahead, he saw that he was almost at the top of Lao Shan.

Now he must bring his bundles. Cautiously he recrossed the sloping cliff.

The carrying pole with bundles attached might trip him, he decided. So he carefully loosed the bundles from it. He wondered if he could throw the bamboo poles across. He made a trial of one of them. It landed safely and did not rebound. He threw the other one. Then the carrying pole. Not a grain of soil escaped from the mat! He threw the bedding roll. Then the clothing.

Now to cross again himself. With the precious bundle of food in his right hand, Li Lun clung to the bushes with his left. Putting his right foot ahead to safe footing, he braced the bundle against it until he could move his left foot forward. Every move he made he guarded. On the last step his right foot slipped a little, but the bushes held firmly.

Li Lun lifted the food to the ledge and pulled himself up beside it. Gratefully he sat down among his belongings. He looked out over the dark green sea. The sea that he had conquered from high places.

" 'There are other things than fishing!' " Sun Ling's words sounded in his ears above the swell of waves against the rocks far below.

Hurriedly Li Lun retied his bundles to the poles. Then, with a lighter heart, he shouldered the poles and set off again, whistling.

A short way ahead the mountaintop looked as if it had been scooped out. There stood a rocky wall to the right as high as an ocean wave. To the left the wall was only as tall as a sampan. Between the two walls was the rocky mountain floor, about as wide as a fishing boat is long.

Crawling along the narrow ledge

At last he had reached the top!

But what a reception! Gulls screeched and screamed all about him.

Dropping his bundles, Li Lun walked cautiously toward the sky wall so that he would know what was beyond. Sharp and rugged rocks bit at his feet. He did not go near the edge of the cliff, which sloped abruptly down into the sea. That was the door which the gulls used, coming and going.

Deep blue and purple shadows had already settled over the face of the water, but the light rays still brightened the mountaintop.

Where would he sleep? Not a blade of grass or a bush was in sight. Only screaming gulls and rock holes. Rock holes with water in them!

Li Lun walked around, looking for a ledge under which he could crawl for shelter. He could not sleep out in the open. The gulls would think that he was a rock and roost on him!

The wind blew chill through the sea-gull door. Li Lun pulled his padded jacket about him more tightly as he walked along the low wall. There was not a spot where he could sleep. He crossed over to the higher wall and continued his search.

Dark gradually closed in about him, like a gray mist creeping up from the blackening waters.

Then he noticed that the gulls were investigating his bundles. Had they smelled the rice? he wondered. Or the shrimp? They might peck holes in the cloth. Hurriedly he stumbled across the rocky floor and drove them away.

When he looked up again, Li Lun saw a dark shadow along the opposite high wall. It was only waist-high, but he struggled over the uneven surface to examine its possibilities.

Sure enough, it was an opening into the rock! Gulls flew out as Li Lun climbed up.

"You will have to find another place to sleep!" challenged Li Lun. "I need this spot, and it is too dark to hunt another."

The cave was about as deep as he was tall, and it had a smaller opening on the face of the rock.

Li Lun pushed the gulls' eggs to the wall of the small cave and dragged over his bundles. He opened his bedroll and, hugging the bundle of rice with both arms, sank exhausted upon his strange bed.

NIGHT

Li Lun awoke suddenly and sat upright. His heart was pounding with fright. Something had awakened him but he did not know what. It might have been a gull trying to get on the ledge. Or it might have been a rat. A stiff south wind was blowing over the low wall and he felt chilly.

The sack of rice was still beside him. He felt for the bundle of clothing and the poles. All were safe. He lay down again and tried hard to sleep.

But such a parade of things as ran through his mind! First, the pig. One of the island pigs had come grunting into their house that morning. Pigs coming into a house brought bad luck. His father had chased it out quickly, muttering, "We don't need ill fortune on our fishing trip!"

Had the pig brought ill fortune for the fishing trip? wondered Li Lun. Or had it brought the bad luck that had sent him up the mountain to grow rice upon the rocky top of Lao Shan?

He thought about that until a rat ran over his foot. Then it occurred to him that he could put up a mat to keep out the wind and the rats. He rose to his knees and felt the left side of the ledge. There was a ridge facing the rock which would hold a pole. He ran his hands over the rocks to the right of the cave. A jut of rock stuck out a little way.

There was a flutter of wings and a cry of distress. That jut of rock had been the roosting place of several sea gulls.

Li Lun caught up one of the bamboo poles and placed it as his curtain rod. Over the rod he hung the mat which had carried the soil. "Now," he thought, "perhaps both the rats and the bad thoughts will stay outside."

He would not take the dragon bones yet. He might need them worse later. Besides, he was not really afraid.

Li Lun lay down again. For a while he thought about the gulls. Now and again one of them screamed. As if it were having bad dreams, Li Lun decided. Perhaps the rats were bothering the gulls, too.

So many things made fear sounds. Going to sleep alone in the cave was not so easy as sleeping on the mat at home with his father and mother near. There, if spirits were around making noises, his mother chased them away. Here, there was no one to help him shove back the night. The wind moaned above the mat and rushed into the cave like something running. But there was nothing he could do about that until the sun came again—except to dread the dark. The frightening sounds made his heart pound heavily. Something scraped against the bamboo poles. His heart raced at the thought of what it might be. Was that the wind, too?

Li Lun shivered as with the cold, though the night was too warm to be chilly. He wondered if perhaps he should take some of the dragon bones. If only he had Ming, with her soft fur and yellow eyes, for company. Almost he felt her fur and heard her purring. What were all of them at home doing? he wondered.

It seemed as if he heard his mother saying the words, "Remember, Li Lun, you are not afraid!" And Sun Ling, "Inner Spirit will keep you strong!" No, he would not need the dragon bones this time.

He thought of spirits flying around. But they could not get into his cave. They would have to turn a corner to do that, and spirits could fly only in a straight line. Still, he pulled his knees up under his chin to make himself as small as possible.

The quieter he tried to lie, the more furiously the wind blew upon Lao Shan. Its howling and blowing made Li Lun recall the story which all the island people knew—the story about the wind and the water and Lao Shan. Lao Shan had once been called Mei Shan—Beautiful Mountain. Mei Shan had grown proud. Proud of being the tallest thing about. Taller than the sea and taller than the wind. The mountain bragged about its tallness until the wind and the sea whispered together and decided to destroy it. They would put the proud old mountain under the sea where all vain things belonged.

Mei Shan laughed at them. The trees on its sides waved their arms playfully in the breezes and birds sang in the branches.

The sun hid itself behind dark clouds and for days did not shine. The winds from all over the earth rolled themselves into huge, black clouds and hung above Mei Shan. Angry waves from the sea rose up to meet the winds. Together the winds and the waves lashed and tore at Mei Shan until everything on it was destroyed. The grass and the trees were uprooted. The ground was washed into the sea. Houses and people were swept into deep waters. Of all the families that had lived on the sides of Mei Shan only two were saved. They had hidden themselves in a cave.

The mountain itself stood firm. But, because its beauty had been washed away, from that time on the people of the island called it Lao Shan — Sorrow Mountain.

Li Lun thought about the name as he huddled in the little shelter. Never had his arms and legs been so cramped. Never had fear thoughts stayed with him for so long. And never had he been so happy to see the morning light.

He pulled down the mat and ran to look over the low wall.

The sea was still living and moving in great swells. It was blue and purple, streaked with rosy promise of a sunshiny day. It was not angry at Lao Shan. Nor would it be angry with the fishermen today. Peace breathed across its broad, smiling face.

Li Lun raised his eyes to the heavens. The sun had not yet risen, but how beautiful the sky! Purple and blue changing to red, to pink. Dawn had not yet reached its fingers to the island below. Gray mist shadows from the sea blanketed it. But here on the mountaintop the light of dawn touched everything!

PLANTING

Suddenly Li Lun realized that he was pinched with hunger. He had not opened the rice sack when he had reached the mountaintop last night. He had been too happy over his safe arrival to think of food. And so exhausted that he had wished only to rest.

Now he smacked his lips in anticipation as he untied the sack. Something to eat! He took a handful of the brown rice kernels. His eyes grew big with surprise. Dried squid was mixed with the rice. And shrimp and seaweed!

"Precious mother!" he murmured as he touched his lips to it. Tears came as he remembered how she had looked at him before he left home. Could that be only yesterday? His heart beat lighter as he munched the unexpected delicacies.

Li Lun was eager to plant the rice. Four moon changes was a long time. He could not get started too soon. But if one must work, one must likewise eat. While he chewed the kernels, he would look for places where he might plant the rice.

Taking another handful of the rice grains, he set the sack back in the cave. Then he walked about, looking first for sticks or reeds to place at the bottom of the rock hole. The growing rice plants would need something to which they could hold fast.

In an old gull nest Li Lun found some weeds. In another nest he found reeds. He leaped about from rock to rock until he had collected enough.

The sun was rising from the water. Its blue and purple changed to gray and green. A gentle breeze came through the Gulls' Doorway. Li Lun sniffed the briny air and threw back his shoulders. It was good to be alive on a mountaintop!

Now he was ready to search for just the right rock hole in which to grow his grains. Back and forth he walked, spying out every place where the gulls nested. He found three spots along the low wall which might grow rice. But the force of the wind coming over the wall would uproot the rice. The Old One had told him that the basin must not be too shallow. So he began his search along the high wall. He looked as far toward the Gulls' Doorway as he dared go.

About halfway between the door and his cave was just what Sun Ling would have ordered. But it was as high as the top of his head above the rocks. There were toe holds to climb up.

"I might stumble and break a leg," he pondered. So he searched along the wall, past his cave, all the way to the stony path which led down the mountain.

As he searched, Li Lun noticed that there was one spot which seemed to be more sheltered than the others.

After looking carefully at several spots he came back to the sheltered one. It was shoulder-high above the rocky floor, and the sun shone on it all day. A mother gull sat there brooding her babies.

"I must have this rock hole for my rice grains!" Li Lun informed her. "Sun Ling said it must look toward the sunshine."

He measured its distance from his cave and found that it was only fifteen man-sized strides.

"That is good," he declared. "Yes, it must be this rock hole!"

He shoved the bird from her nest. "Sorry, Mrs. Gull, but you must give it to me."

The gull answered by flying at Li Lun's face and trying to peck out his eyes. Li Lun shielded them with the crook of his elbow. Cautiously he looked and saw two babies in the nest.

The mother gull came closer and struck at him so fiercely that he had to move away. He went back to the cave to pick up a pole. Then, fighting off the gull, he moved her babies to another rock hole. But he had to leave for a while. She would not let him go ahead with his planting.

The Old One had told him to mix with the soil some bird droppings for fertilizer. So Li Lun took a large, flat stone and gathered from the rocks as much as Sun Ling had told him to use.

When he returned to the rock hole, the mother gull did not appear. Her babies were crying and trying to get out of their new home, which was narrower than the old one had been. Li Lun wondered if the mother had gone for food.

He set about mixing the soil with bird droppings. Then he placed the weeds at the bottom of the rock hole and covered them with the soil from Sun Ling's garden. He breathed a blessing for the kindly old man with hair like a white cloud in the sunshine.

Without warning the mother gull struck at Li Lun's eyes. He shielded them with his arms and grabbed at the bird.

"Over here are your chicks!" he called as he ran to the spot where he had placed the young ones. But the mother flew away with other birds that were circling about, protesting his presence.

"I shall have to find another mother for you," said Li Lun as he watched the struggles of the gull chicks. The new nest was waist-high above the floor. But there were rats around, and rats could easily jump that distance if the mother bird was not on guard. He would see to this later. Now he must plant his rice.

Li Lun went back to his rice rock. He reached into his deep

The mother gull struck at Li Lun

pocket. One by one he took the grains from it and planted them deep in the rich soil. Beside each covered grain he stuck a gull feather. He took off his padded jacket and threw it over the soil to keep away the birds. Then he took a gourd dipper and went in search of water to flood the paddy field.

By now the sun was overhead. It beat down upon him. Perspiration trickled down his face and neck as he trudged back and forth with his dipper of water.

Li Lun wondered where the fishermen were. How happy he was that he was not out on the deep sea!

Suddenly Li Lun realized that he was very hungry. He had drunk water but that did not serve as food. He washed his hands, one at a time, by pouring water from the dipper. Then he took a handful of food from the sack and went over to the low wall. There he could look at the sea as he ate.

Li Lun liked to watch the sea crawling and fighting the land. He saw below him the surf pounding against the rocks of Lao Shan. It rushed up and fell back, then came again. He leaned over the wall. Sun Ling's shack was just at the edge down there. But Li Lun could not see it for the trees.

The food in his hand was gone. It was not lonely to eat by oneself, reflected Li Lun, if one could gaze upon the sea from a distance. He got up and stretched himself. He was tired from climbing up and down the rocks for water. But the rice must be kept flooded. Sun Ling had warned him that it took much water for both the reeds and the soil to soak up enough.

Hour after hour Li Lun worked. It was short-shadow time before he stopped to rest again. "I am tired enough to sleep with my head stuck into a rock corner, like those baby gulls," he told the water.

When everything was finished for the day he said aloud, "I wish Sun Ling could see my rice field now!" Proudly he dipped his finger into the water above the planted grains.

That night no fears tormented Li Lun. The darkness and the aloneness held fewer terrors for him. The wind whispered soft songs from the sea. Bad spirits stayed under the deep sea water where they belonged. If rats were around, they did not get behind his curtain, and the gull cries did not startle him out of his wits. They were simply shouting warnings to one another, he decided. Perhaps telling of a new fishing ground they had discovered. Men did the same things.

The next day, and the next, Li Lun had to carry more and more water. The rice must be kept flooded. And how thirsty the sun was!

Hour after hour Li Lun sat and watched for fear the gulls would get his rice grains. Almost from daylight to dark he stood guard over them, except when he was carrying water from the rock holes.

On the fourth day Li Lun saw tiny green sprouts pushing

their heads above the soil. He stared at them unbelievingly.

"It is true!" he marveled. "I can grow rice as my grandfather did, years ago!" He hopped up and down in front of his precious plants.

"If only my father could see! If only my mother could see! If only Sun Ling could see!"

He looked up into the sky to tell the wind, the sun — yes, the clouds, too. The sun had hidden itself. But the wind was there. And the clouds were there, so close upon him that they pressed their mists into his face.

And the clouds did water his plants. They watered his plants for three whole days. They filled all the rock holes with water. For three whole days Li Lun rested from his water-carrying and let the clouds keep his rice field flooded.

But Li Lun was not idle. "I shall have to make a pile of stones," he told himself, "to tell how many days are passing." Between showers he collected stones for his calendar. He placed a pile of them just outside the cave. With the beginning of every day he put one inside the cave on his calendar rock pile. "One hundred and twenty days for ripening," Sun Ling had said. "Keep much water on the plants for thirty days."

Suddenly Li Lun heard a squawking from the baby gulls. When he looked, he saw a rat running away with one of the babies in its mouth. He hurried over to the nest.

"That mother gull is not looking after you very well," he

told the remaining one as it shivered against the gray rocks. "I shall bring my shirt to cover you."

He ran to get it. "There, now the rats will not find you. I shall look after you, if your mother does not. You shall be my pet gull!"

He tucked the blue shirt around the quaking little chick. Over the rock hole he set up the bamboo pole flying the red paper. "For good luck," he told the baby gull.

Then he went out to chase a mother gull or two from her nest. "I must find some eggs to feed the baby gull if its mother is going to neglect it," he said aloud.

But when Li Lun returned with two eggs for the little chick, he discovered that the rat had been there before him. There was no baby chick. There was only the blue shirt in the rock hole.

Li Lun put his arm across his eyes and hugged the shirt. A sob choked him. Not even a baby gull for a pet! He walked slowly over to his rice patch for comfort.

MILDEW

Each morning Li Lun ate his breakfast to the sound of the North Temple bells on Lo Shan. He took a handful of food and perched himself on Gulls' Roost, his name for a flat rock in the low wall. There, as he nibbled the brown rice kernels, he watched the day take a fresh start. Gulls were already winging their way seaward.

How alive the water! It never tired of running and leaping. Sampans, freighters from foreign lands, junks, houseboats, and smaller craft filled the sea lanes. Dark, low-hanging clouds sailed swiftly before warm southeast breezes.

When Li Lun saw the moon growing big and round and full he counted the stones in his calendar. There were many—he had been on the mountaintop one moon change. Through three more moon changes he would have to tend his rice plants and guard over them.

They had grown so tall that he could no longer cover them with his jacket, for fear of breaking the stems. He must think of another way to keep the birds away while he went for water. The plants did not need quite so much water now. Sun Ling had told him that the stems did not have to be covered. But Li Lun knew that the toes of the rice plants must still be kept well under water.

He sat down to think how he could protect the plants from the greedy gulls. He looked at the bamboo pole with the piece of red paper flying from the end of it. Then he glanced at the other pole, lying beside the rock at his feet.

"I know!" he cried as he jumped down and picked it up. "I will fasten my shirt to this pole. It will flap in the breezes and frighten the birds away."

Carefully Li Lun fastened his blue shirt to the pole. It flapped joyously above the rice plants, and to Li Lun's delight the gulls did not come near. Picking up the dipper, he bounded from one rock pile to another for water. Some of the holes were so shallow that he had to use his hand to scoop the water into the dipper.

Everywhere gulls scolded him, flew at him, and tried to frighten him. He waved them aside. When he had no water in the dipper, he brandished his arms and scolded back.

To and fro he went, carrying water to his precious rice plants.

"Be sure you hold full measure water for my plants," he told the rocks. "I must honor my most venerable grandfather's soul by growing these seven grains of rice."

Li Lun thought of the fishermen. He wondered if they were catching many fish. "How thankful I am for the chance to grow rice — even among rocks!" he breathed.

At last he sat on the rock outside his cave. "I have carried water until I am tired," he sighed. Leaning his head against the cave rock he was soon fast asleep.

Hours later Li Lun awakened, hungry. Yet he sat for a moment, marveling at the silence of the mountain. This was a place where one could think! Even the wind was soft with lovely whisperings. The gulls were sleeping peacefully. No dogs baying at the moon, no cats telling their troubles to the village, no pigs squealing or grunting. And no smelly fish along the shore.

"I must eat something," Li Lun told the night as he hugged his padded jacket tighter. He took as many rice grains as he had fingers and sat down to gaze at the twinkling stars. Still weary, he fell sound asleep before he ate a single grain.

A gull lighting on his shoulder awakened him. It was morning, though the temple bells had not yet rung.

As was his custom, Li Lun took a handful of rice from the sack and settled himself upon Gulls' Roost. The taste of the kernels caused him to blow the food into space.

"Mildew!" he cried. "Mildew has found where I keep my

Watering the precious rice plants

food hidden!" he protested to the sun as it climbed from the water.

Mildew in his food! Whatever would he do? All of it would be ruined, useless! He was frightened at the thought of it. Then he remembered his mother's asking him if he knew what to do in case the rice became mildewed. And how happy he had been to reply that he did know, that Sun Ling had told him what to do.

Sun Ling, the wise man at the foot of the mountain, had said, "Spread the mildewed rice on a mat in the sun. The sun will eat the mildew."

But Li Lun could not spread the rice in the sun until he had carried water for the plants. The sun would shrivel the rice to a brown wisp.

Quickly he put up the pole with the shirt flying in the breezes. Then in the cool of the morning he clambered up and down the rocks. His stomach was empty, but he was no longer frightened. Faintly he sang:

"The sun will eat the mildew,
And I can eat the food."

When the rice was plentifully supplied with water, Li Lun emptied the food sack carefully upon the mat which served as the cave door. He could not leave the food for an instant, for the sharp-eyed gulls circled overhead constantly.

Li Lun's eyes caught sight of the stone pile. "I will throw

stones at you," he shouted to the daring gulls, "if you do not keep away!"

Whenever a gull flew low to settle, Li Lun whizzed a stone at it. What a squawking and shrieking! Not only from the gull that was hit, but from all the neighbor gulls that happened to be back from the sea. Occasionally one would sit on a rock near by, waiting for a chance to find Li Lun asleep. But Li Lun's eyes were wide, wide open.

Every few moments he turned the rice and sea foods. When the sun was ove head, he packed it again in the bags and returned them to the cave.

"Now my food is safe once more!" he said thankfully.

That day, as on other days, when the plants were watered and when no gulls were flying near, Li Lun leaned out over the rocks and looked far down upon the village below. Often, when it was not misty and after his eyes became accustomed to the distance, he could see people walking about. Always he hoped to be able to catch a glimpse of his mother or of his little brothers. But, strain as he would, he could not tell who the tiny figures were.

A VISITOR

One morning Li Lun did not waken until long after the ringing of the Temple bells. The sun was high in the sky. With the suddenness of an alarm bell he dashed out of his cave and rushed over to his plants. Frantically he hoped the gulls had forgotten about the rice.

But the gulls were wise. When they did not see the red paper and the blue shirt fluttering, they came to investigate. No one was there to drive them away. They circled closer, determined to find out what this stuff was from which they had been kept away. It was green, so it must be good to eat. They pecked at the stalks until they pulled out two by the roots. But these plants did not have the juicy bulbous roots of the swamp plants, so they dropped them. Circling round again, since there still was no one to drive them away, they came back just for the fun of pulling more plants.

But then Li Lun had wakened. He picked up stones as he ran and shied them at the disappearing gulls.

Fearfully Li Lun stepped up on the rock to view his plants. He leaned over them, and a cry escaped his lips.

"Oh, Oh!" he breathed. "The gulls have taken two!" With his fingers he dug into the soil, wondering if they had left the roots. Li Lun bit his lips to keep back sobs which choked his throat. The roots were gone, too.

Looking around, he discovered one broken rice plant near by. He picked it up and carried it tenderly back to his rice rock. With his fingers he made a hole big enough to hold the plant. When he had the roots firmly anchored he tried to prop up the stem. But it was no use. It was broken in two places and drooped its head.

Li Lun was almost ill over the loss of the plants. All day he mourned as he shied away the gulls. But he went to bed earlier than usual that evening, knowing that he must not over-sleep again.

The next morning he looked up to thank the clouds for their help. It had rained. The rice patch was flooded, and the five plants stood firm and green. For several days he would not have to carry water.

He put a handful of the rice in his pocket and chewed it for his breakfast as he went about collecting stones and adding to his food supply whenever he found unprotected gulls' nests with eggs. And when he discovered a swiftlet's nest that was low enough for him to reach, he pulled it down and dried it for the shopkeepers' supply.

It was near the short-shadow hour that Li Lun was coming up the trail. He turned suddenly and listened, for he thought he heard someone behind him. The gulls were screeching even more than usual, and below loose rocks were clattering down the approach.

Li Lun hid behind one of the ledges as he caught the sound of footsteps coming nearer. Warily he thrust out his head, then held his breath as he saw the small round black cap and knee-length black coat of a priest. He was one of the priests of the North Temple. His loose yellow trousers were bound below the knees by cloth puttees. He wore stout mountain shoes and carried a staff to help himself up the steep trail.

The priest looked up and caught sight of the boy. He seemed almost as surprised as Li Lun.

The Good One clambered up the path until he was close to Li Lun. Then he stopped and faced the boy.

"Are you in trouble?" he asked.

"I?" questioned Li Lun greatly surprised. He thought a moment. He was in trouble enough. But what kind of trouble did the priest mean? Could the womenfolk on the island have told the Good One why he was there?

"You have a flag waving now and again," the priest said.

"Oh!" Li Lun was relieved. "That is my shirt," he explained. "I hung it on the pole—"

But now what to say! He pinched his toes together and looked down at them. To say that his shirt was waving gulls away from seven, no, five poor little rice plants—that would sound silly. He could not tell that to the good priest, the Keeper of the North Temple. Or, maybe—could he?

Together the priest and Li Lun continued the climb up the mountain trail. Soon they came to the rocks where the blue shirt was waving over the precious rice plants.

"Why are you staying up here?" asked the priest, looking from the bamboo pole and the shirt to the cave where he could see many gulls' eggs stored.

"I—I—" Li Lun started, then stopped. But he must tell the Good One something! So he had best tell him the truth. Find it out soon or late, he would anyway.

"I—" he began again, then stammered. "I—am a coward, most honorable Father of the Temple."

Li Lun twisted his fingers around the bamboo pole and looked at his feet.

The priest waited patiently.

Finally Li Lun looked up into the Good One's kindly round face. Those deep-set understanding brown·eyes could be trusted with his secret. His smile encouraged Li Lun.

"You see, most honorable Keeper of the Temple, I did not

"You are brave," the Good One tells Li Lun

go fishing with my father and the menfolk because — because I am afraid. Afraid of the sea water." There! He had it out!

The priest did not answer. Just stood with his hand shading his eyes, looking out over the sea.

"They will call me a coward always." Li Lun's voice trembled near tears.

The Good One turned and faced the boy. "You still have not told me why you are up here."

"My father sent me," confessed Li Lun. "He commanded me to grow seven grains of rice to a head. Up here he said I would be far enough away from sea water."

"Ah, rice!" exclaimed the priest looking earnestly at Li Lun. "Where is your rice?"

"Here." The boy pointed to the rock corner. "Beside this rock, Father. The gulls pulled two out this morning because I overslept. This one and one that they carried away. This one has a broken stem." Li Lun trembled with eagerness.

"So it is coward's work to grow rice at the top of a mountain," mused the Good One, examining the broken rice plant.

"Yes, most honorable Keeper of the Temple," answered Li Lun humbly.

"Rice has not been grown on Lao Shan for many years. This is a fishing island. No one has even tried to grow rice since the destruction of Mei Shan."

"Yes, most honorable Father."

For a long time the priest was silent as he continued to look full at Li Lun, then at the little rice patch. At last he spoke.

"Would a man be a coward who could create a mountain like Lao Shan or Lo Shan?" the black-robed man asked.

"Ah, no!" breathed Li Lun softly. "He would be a great man. That would be wonder work."

"The wise men of old," the Good One told Li Lun, "have ever said that 'the production of a grain of rice is as great a work as the creation of a mountain.'"

He placed his hand on Li Lun's shoulder. "What is your name, rice grower?"

"I am Li Lun from the Village of the Three Fir Trees, most honorable Father."

"And you think you are a coward," the priest said kindly. "You have tended the rice, you have watered it faithfully, you have guarded it from the birds. . . . You are no coward! You are brave, Li Lun. Braver than if you had gone fishing."

For a moment Li Lun thought that an earthquake had shaken the mountain. His knees were weak and trembling. He tried to smile at the priest, but the smile only made hurt tears come to his eyes.

"Bring the rice to me when it is ripe," the Good One commanded Li Lun. "We shall have a temple ceremony for it."

RAIN

For days Li Lun was in the midst of rain clouds. Sometimes it was only a mist and a drizzle. Again there was such a downpour, accompanied by high winds, that Li Lun had to stay inside his small cave to keep from being soaked to the skin. It was the sixth month — the season of great rains.

Li Lun learned that during heavy rains and high winds the gulls did not disturb his plants. When the mist lay thick upon the mountain, they did not seem to know that the rice was there. Through their doorway they followed the sea. So Li Lun had more time upon his hands. So much free time that he grew stiff, trying to prop up his backbone in his cave shelf during all the rain.

"I shall build beauty with my hands," Li Lun told the rain clouds when they shut out the sun so that he could see nothing. "I shall build a rock seat over in the Gulls' Doorway.

Then I can watch the gulls come and go in the mist, and when the skies clear I can look upon the sea from a bench.

The heavy mist did not keep Li Lun from working. He decided upon a spot about three of his own lengths from the open doorway. Stones which were too large to carry he rolled over and over until he had them properly set. The flat pieces he laid aside for the top of the bench.

Day after day in the mist Li Lun carried stones. Small ones he dropped on the calendar pile. Very small ones went to chink in the hollows between larger stones. Most of these he collected from the ledge pathway that led down the mountainside.

While carrying rocks, he found a large rock hole almost hidden in a cleft of rock. The sun could not find that rock hole. Li Lun swept it clean with his hands, then filled it with water from overflowing rock holes.

"I may need that water later," he told the dipper. "It is my very own supply."

When the rain became drenching, Li Lun had to run to the cave for shelter. He kept the mat across the entrance constantly so that driving rains would not moisten his food and cause it to mildew again.

Then for three days he was kept in his cave. The rain splashed against the rocks and gurgled toward the Gulls' Doorway. There it streamed down into the sea. Setting the dipper against the rocks, Li Lun collected enough water for drinking and for washing his hands. At the end of the third day he could endure this sort of life no longer. He must see how his rice plants were faring.

But how to get to his paddy and back without getting soaked? His clothing would never dry in weather like this!

"Inner Spirit!" something whispered to him. "You know the gulls do not touch the plants when it rains. Content yourself within this small house. You do not need to see the rice now. Wait until the rain ceases."

Li Lun smiled to himself. "The rice plants are happy. It rains for them."

He followed his thoughts to the high seas where the fisherfolk were. Was it raining out there? Were they waiting, the tarpaulin pulled over them from bow to stern, until the rain ceased — even as he waited in his small shelter? Or, since it had been raining such a long time, had they come back to Blue Shark Island?

Li Lun wondered if his father would climb the mountain to seek him. He recalled how angry Teng Lun had been and decided that he need not expect his father to struggle up Lao Shan. Teng Lun thought his son was a coward. Teng Lun did not know that a man who grew rice did a noble work.

Then Li Lun went home with his thoughts. The cold rain made teeth chatter in the home shack, too. In the center of the room the brothers and little sister would be gathered around the floor tile in which they burned weeds, sticks, and paper for warmth. The cats would look wise from their places on the benches. Perhaps Teng Lun would be mending nets in the corner, with the ducks waddling about his feet, examining every bit of fiber and rope which dropped to the floor for possible food. And pigs would be trying the door now and again with grunts and squeals, hoping to get out of the rain. Beautiful Mother would be getting the rice cakes ready with seaweed. There would be hot tea, made with water caught from the roof of the house. Oh, how delicious that would be!

Li Lun shivered with cold as tears welled into his eyes. He shook himself and held the door mat tighter.

One by one he counted the days of his calendar since it had begun to rain. "Half a moon change," he sighed.

The rain was still so heavy that Li Lun could not look for stones to complete the stone bench. "I must make a doll and hang it on the left of the Gulls' Doorway!" he exclaimed. "A doll of the girl-who-sweeps-clear-the-weather. I grow pale when the sun does not shine. The rice grows yellow when the daystar does not come for so long."

Li Lun looked questioningly at the bundles, at his bedroll, and at his clothing. What could he use in making the doll? His mother always used paper, but he had no paper. One of the small bags which held his food supply was almost empty. That bag would make the girl-who-sweeps-clear-the-weather! He emptied the remaining rice into the full bag.

Li Lun took a stone from the rock pile and twisted the bottom of the bag around it for a head. He loosed a fiber from the edge of his hat and wrapped it into a neck. He pulled two strips from the end of the bedroll and twisted them into arms and legs. The top of the bag hung loose for the skirt. With a stiff reed he marked eyes, nose, and mouth on the head and held it up for inspection. Then he fastened another cord about the neck so that the doll might hang and look out through the Gulls' Doorway. She would be ashamed of the weather. She would sweep the sky clear.

Li Lun wondered how he could get the clear-weather girl to the Gulls' Doorway without getting drenched. "I will wear the door mat! It will be for only a minute. You be a good girl now and sweep the skies clear," Li Lun told her.

He took down the door mat and draped it over his head. With his trousers rolled above his knees he looked like an upside-down U as he darted out into the rain.

When he reached the Gulls' Doorway, he could find no place to hang the doll. So he picked up a stone and set it on top of the cord which he had tied around her neck. This held her on the ledge and let her swing out from it. Swaying in the wind and rain, she whirled as if the storm were made for dancing.

A gull flew down and pecked at her arms.

"Keep away!" shouted Li Lun waving his arms frantically. "Must you grab at everything you see? She is to sweep the weather clear."

The gull squawked as if he cried, "Oh! Oh! Keep the weather clear!"

And other gulls answered, "Keep the weather clear! Oh! Oh!"

RATS

After the third moon change the girl-who-sweeps-clear-the-weather brushed things so well that Li Lun was sorry he had hung out the doll. The mountain was parched. The sun was so scorching that the rice seemed to dry up rather than to grow. The hot ball of fire licked the water right out of the rock bowl in which the rice was planted. It was dry, too, on the island below the mountain. When Li Lun looked down upon the village he saw that the leaves on the camphorwood trees and on the tea bushes had a hard, brownish look.

"The sun drinks faster than I can carry," sighed Li Lun. "I must find something that will give shade to the roots. The rocks are hot as fever. I fear that the heat coming from them will burn the plants."

Li Lun looked at his jacket, but it was no' to give much shade to the plants. He thought of t had carried the soil. He went to the cave and brought it to the rice patch.

The plants had been growing through three moon changes. They were now knee-high. If he stood the mat around them, it would be sure to blow over on the tops of the rice and break the stems. Besides, he could not reach up over the mat to the soil.

Li Lun stood and looked first at the plants, then at the mat. There was only one way to give the rice shade. That was to hang the mat from the rocks above and weight it down with heavy stones. While the mat hung there, it would shut out the sun from the rice patch. Li Lun decided that during the hottest hours of the day he would protect the plants from the sun's heat in this way.

"And when the mat is hanging there, it will keep you gulls away. I will not have to fly the shirt to scare you off," he told a pair of gulls that flew too near.

As soon as Li Lun had the mat in position, he took a dipper and started in search of water. Finding water was becoming more and more difficult, for it had not rained in a whole moon change. Each day Li Lun had to go farther down the mountain to find rock holes with water in them.

When he had collected enough water in his dipper for the plants, he dragged himself slowly up the mountainside. By the time he reached the top he was so thirsty that he had to take veral sips of the water he had gathered with such difficulty.

Then he poured what remained into the rock hole behind the mat.

When the sun was low in the sky, Li Lun climbed up to remove the stones and let the mat drop down. Then he looked to see if there were enough water on the plants.

For a moment he was so shocked that he stood motionless.

"The rats!" he exclaimed. "The rats have gnawed the stems!"

Jumping to the rocky floor he picked up the three stems that had been chewed off a little way above the roots. "My rice!" he mourned. "My precious rice!" His hands trembled, he was so angry. Now what would he do? What would he have to show his father? But the priest at the temple would understand what had happened. He had climbed the mountain and had seen the rats.

Li Lun examined the seed pods. Every grain had been eaten. He gathered the stems and the few green husks that still remained. Tenderly he put them on a ledge in the cave. Then he went back to see what he could do about the two remaining stalks.

"I will not put up the sleeping mat again," he told himself. "The rats would not dare touch the plants in the sunlight. Rice, you must take your chances against the sun."

His heart was heavy with the loss of the three plants. Yet, he figured, if all went well with the remaining two, he might still have seven times as many grains as he had planted. But he must keep the gulls and rats away. He would put up the shirt whenever he went for water and hope that with no mat to protect them the rats would behave themselves.

It grew harder and harder to find water. Many times Li Lun was tempted to go to the shadow rock hole and give that water to the rice plants. But always Inner Spirit talked to him. "Go farther down the mountain. You will need the shadow water later!"

Another thing worried Li Lun. The squid, shrimp, and seaweed he had eaten long ago. Only a little rice remained in his food bag. He must take a few grains less each day and chew it longer to make it last through the fourth moon change. And he must hunt and find more gulls' eggs to eat with the rice.

"If only I can bring the two plants to head. Then I will have what my father commanded."

Li Lun fell to thinking of his father. He thought of Teng Lun as he had seen him last. Standing beside his fishing sampan with clenched fists, hurt and angry and not knowing whether to strike or not. The taunts from the boys in the other sampans sounded in Li Lun's ears so clearly that he felt he could never forget them. And those boys who had called him coward had been his friends, too!

Then Li Lun thought of the priest from the North Temple and he repeated aloud the Good One's words: "You are no

70

coward! You are brave, Li Lun. Braver than if you had gone fishing."

The picture of silver-haired Sun Ling sitting on the bench beside him encouraged Li Lun, too. And he remembered what the Old One had said: "Your name, Li, means Inner Spirit. That will keep you strong!"

DROUGHT

Anxiously Li Lun watched the grain heads as they developed. Besides the gulls and the rats, the sun also was now an enemy of the grain. It drank the water Li Lun poured upon the rice faster than the plants could drink it. And water was so hard to find! From sunrise to the hour of short shadows Li Lun worked to find sometimes only a half-dipperful. He searched until he was exhausted. Each day he had to travel farther. But there was also gain. On the longer trips he always came back with gulls' eggs in his shirt pockets.

The few shrubs and weeds on the mountainside were now seared brown. The rocks were hot to touch. Li Lun had to keep his sandals on his feet constantly during the days. At night, when he curled up in his cave, it was a relief to take them off. He hung them carefully from the ledge so that the rats would not find them and chew them up. He had to guard against that, for he could not walk on the hot rocks without them, and he had nothing out of which he could make others.

The water in the special shadow rock hole where the sun could not reach he saved for himself. Saved it against the time when the thirsty sun would have drunk all the water in the other rock holes.

One morning a great calm settled over the sea. Li Lun watched it from the rice rock as he fastened the blue shirt to the bamboo pole and set it up. The shirt hung tired and limp.

"I know how you feel, little shirt," Li Lun told the blue rag. "I feel tired, too. Almost I cannot breathe. It is so hot!" He wiped the trickling perspiration from his face. "But I must find some water. See, the plants are drooping their heads. The grains are getting ripe and heavy."

Li Lun looked around him. Not a gull was to be seen. "It is too hot even for gulls to be flying around," he said aloud. "Today I will get the water from the rock hole in the shadows. Then I will not be gone long."

He drank a little himself—hardly enough to quench his thirst. He wished that he could stay there where the sun could not torment him. But he must not. The gulls might return and get the rice grains.

He took enough in the dipper to water the remaining stalks. "Just a little drink for each of you," he whispered, "from my very own water supply."

Li Lun had been gone only a very little while. But when he returned, he stared at the rice rock unbelievingly. For there stood not two stalks of rice — but one. Only one stalk of rice! Even the husks were gone. No gulls were about.

"A rat!" gasped Li Lun numbly as the water dripped unheeded from his dipper. "It must have been a rat!"

Li Lun felt as if he were standing on his heart down in the bottom of his sandals. It could not be true. Perhaps it was a nightmare and he would waken from it!

After a time he climbed onto the rock and very carefully counted the seed husks on the one remaining plant. When he reached the seven times as many grains, he stopped counting, he was so relieved. There were more, many more. Li Lun breathed again.

Li Lun decided that he would sit beside the rice rock all day. He could still sleep through the dark hours, for nothing had ever disturbed the plants at night.

Four suns later, with the first streaks of dawn, Li Lun hurried to the shadow rock hole to get himself a drink.

"How thankful I am that Inner Spirit directed me to fill the shadow rock hole brimful during the rainy season! Now," pondered Li Lun seriously, "I must choose between guarding the rice from the gulls and the rats and carrying water for the plants."

Watching the gulls, he retraced his steps to the rice rock.

Li Lun stared unbelievingly

"If I go far down the mountain to get water, my one precious rice plant will disappear also. I must guard it above everything!"

Content in his heart that he was doing what had to be done, Li Lun took a few rice kernels from the almost empty food bag and lingered near the rice plant.

From daylight to dusk Li Lun sat in the hot sun, guarding the single stalk of rice. As he watched, he gazed out over the sea. The water looked cool and green. It was not so hot out there as on the mountain, he knew. And there were no rats on the water. No, but there were spirits beneath it. Spirits that could pull a fisherboy out of the sampan and push him under the water. Li Lun shivered.

"I want to live on the land always," he told the sun. "I know how my grandfather felt. He would not go on the water either. I am like him. He grew rice. I will grow rice. I like to grow rice." He touched the plant gently to feel the aliveness of it.

The time for ripening seed must be near. Perhaps he would have to take the grains before they were wholly ripe. He would count the stones of his rock calendar and set them in piles, one pile for each moon change.

While he watched the rice rock, Li Lun counted enough stones for one moon change. Enough for two moon changes. Three moon changes. Stones for half of the fourth moon change, and two stones more.

Li Lun whistled a wind song, he was so happy. It did not matter so much now if the grains dried for lack of water. The head was there with the seed grains in it, and harvest was near. To guard them — that was the important thing!

"I am a grower of rice!" Li Lun told himself proudly. And he repeated aloud what the priest had told him : " 'The production of a grain of rice is as great a work as the creation of a mountain.' " He breathed deeply. It was good to be alive, good to be growing rice upon a mountaintop.

There was food for only two days more. Three days, if he ate less and went hungry to bed. On the third day, Li Lun decided, he must harvest the head of rice.

HARVEST

Early the third morning, before the gulls began circling the mountain on their never-ending search for food, Li Lun was beside his rice plant. It bowed its heads to the breezes, its seeds made heavy by mist and dew.

"I will not pick you until the sun has dried your heads," he murmured as he caressed the grains gently. "Then you can hold them up."

From the cave he took the twelve grains of rice which would be his breakfast and dinner on this last day of his aloneness on the mountain. There was a half-dipper of water, too. Warm water, but he drank it all. Then, taking one kernel of rice at a time, he champed and munched. "I am chewing long enough to be eating four pigs' feet," he chuckled.

He stretched himself on the rock before the cave. "Stomach," he patted it lightly, "do not get hungry today. The new rice is not for us to eat. We have a long walk over rough stones to the North Temple. That is where we go first."

Li Lun was impatient to start for the Temple, yet he was reluctant to harvest his rice plant. He had watched time drag so many hours past it. Now he enjoyed seeing the heads gradually lift as the sun pulled the mists from their husks.

"Did you know that I came four times last night to see if you were all right?" Li Lun asked the rice stalk. "I could not sleep for thinking about taking you to the Temple today. I am going to take you, roots and all. The priest expected me to bring five plants. But he will understand if I bring only one. He has a knowing heart."

At first Li Lun thought he would carry the plant in his hands. Then he feared that some of the grains might fall out. "When it is time to take you, I shall put you into the deep pocket of my padded jacket," he decided.

Li Lun talked on and on as he chewed his rice-grain breakfast. He was overjoyed that it was the day of harvest for him. Happy, too, that he would be returning to his home.

He wondered how many fish the men had brought from the deep sea water. Would they have shrimp and squid, too? He looked down upon the village but it was still sleeping. A few older men — he could not tell who they were — were pulling seaweed to the drying racks.

Li Lun went about getting his belongings ready. He packed·

the birds' nests into the bag which had contained his food supply. His dirty clothing he rolled into a bundle. The bamboo poles he tied to the carrying pole. The gourd dippers he strung about his neck. As he took the small package of dragon bones from the ledge and stuck it into the deep pocket of his coat, he smiled. Not all the fears of the mountain had forced him to open it!

Then he went out to his rice patch. His heart was singing. Now that it was time to go, he could hardly wait to be home again. His mother would cook rice cakes seasoned with shrimp and seaweed. Li Lun's eyes shone brightly at the thought. And his father would be proud when he saw the rice his son had raised!

The long-awaited moment had come. Gently Li Lun pulled the rice plant from the soil. The dirt fell away easily from the roots. Almost, Li Lun thought, as if it were happy that the rice was going to the Temple. "I have told you so many times," he said to it.

Stooping, Li Lun put himself under the pole with its burdens. Then he picked up the rice plant and placed it carefully in his deep pocket. He turned for a last look at the familiar surroundings which for almost four moon changes had been home. How he wished the stone bench could be transported by loving thoughts to his father's door!

"I shall have to leave the bench for you," he told the gulls that circled above. "Good-by, gulls!" Li Lun waved to them. "I will not disturb you again."

He turned from his cave, glad that the long, dreary nights now belonged to the past. The rice repaid him for those nights. Days, he had been so busy caring for the rice plants that the time really had not seemed overlong. He turned and gazed back from the bend in the trail. A lump caught in his throat. The gulls were already claiming the bench and his old sleeping quarters.

With a joyous heart he followed the pathless trail down the mountain. Almost Li Lun had forgotten about the cliff which sloped into the sea. But it held no terrors for him now. He had crossed it too many times with a dipper of water. The green bushes which grew on its rocky surface were now bare scrawny twigs. He grasped them tightly and crossed safely with his full load.

As he picked his way over the rocks he considered how he would get to the Temple without going through the Village of Three Fir Trees. At the foot of the mountain one trail led directly to the village. Another path wound around back of the mountain, between Lao Shan and Lo Shan, and led at last to the Temple.

Li Lun thought that he could get to the Temple without being seen by any of the villagers. It was still early in the day, and few persons visited the Temple until late afternoon.

A few gulls followed him from the mountaintop, as if to

keep him company on his homeward way. They flew ahead of him, then alighted to watch until he caught up. Li Lun wondered if they would miss him. Swiftlets darted from the camphorwood trees up the mountainside and flew to their cliff homes.

When he reached the foot of the mountain, Li Lun sat down on a rock to rest for a moment. Then he straightened up and, taking a deep breath, started on the trail which branched to the right.

Suddenly Li Lun heard voices from behind the mountain. Soon he saw a group of village boys. To his dismay he saw that some of them were boys who had been on the man-making fishing trip.

"Sea-water coward! Sea-water coward!" they jeered as they recognized Li Lun.

Li Lun flushed with anger. They had no right to taunt him. He had been sent to grow rice and he had done his work, just as they had done their fishing.

"Afraid of sea water! Afraid of sea water!"

Li Lun faced them bravely. "I am not a coward," he defended himself. "I have done what I was sent to do!"

By this time all six of them were sing-songing:

"Sea-water coward! Sea-water coward!
Afraid of sea water! Afraid of sea water!"

"Let's throw him into the sea!" one of the boys suggested. They made a dart at Li Lun.

"Sea-water coward," taunted the village boys

But Li Lun was not entirely unprepared. Dropping the carrying pole from his shoulder, he started flaying the bamboo pole right and left, up and down.

The boys were taken completely by surprise. They scattered in all directions to avoid the sudden trouncing. Then, while they planned what to do next, Li Lun climbed under the yoke of the carrying pole and hurried on toward the Temple.

After he had gone a short distance, he glanced over his shoulder. He was dismayed to see that the boys were still following him. With no load to weight them down, they could run faster than he.

Li Lun grabbed the bamboo pole tightly and stumbled ahead. If only he could get around the next bend, he would be in sight of the Temple. He glanced swiftly back to gauge the speed of the boys. They were gaining on him.

Again the sing-song taunts began. Li Lun's heart quickened as he heard them. If they used their breath to hurl coward words, he reasoned, they would have that much less for running.

They had almost reached him when he stumbled through the little gate into the tea grove adjoining the Temple. There, on a stone bench beside the Temple steps, sat a priest. The same priest who had talked to Li Lun on the mountaintop. Gasping for breath, Li Lun stood before him.

"Mountaintop rice grower!" exclaimed the black-robed priest. "I am glad you have come!"

The village boys stopped short when they saw the priest. But they lingered outside the gate and hurled coward threats at Li Lun.

The Good One turned from Li Lun and walked over to them.

"Tell your people to come to the Temple with the long sun shadows today," he commanded. "Tell everyone in the village to come. There is something—" he turned to look at Li Lun crouched at the foot of the Temple steps—"there is something of importance to tell them."

TEMPLE CEREMONY

Li Lun watched anxiously as the boys turned away from the gate. They hurled no more coward words, but they walked backward and sent ugly thoughts with their eyes.

The priest returned to his seat on the bench and beckoned Li Lun to sit beside him.

Li Lun did so gladly. He was weary from hunger and his feet were bruised where sharp stones had torn through his sandals.

"Tell me," asked the Good One, "how much rice did you bring?"

Li Lun reached into his deep pocket and drew from it the rice plant. He gave it to the priest. "Just this one, Good Father, was I able to save for the harvest."

Then, reaching again into his pocket, he pulled out all that remained of the other four plants. "The gulls pulled this one before it was ripe, and one they took that I could not find." Sadly he showed the priest the broken stalks. "I think that rats destroyed these three. See, the heads had already formed. This one was ripe, but the rats ate all the grains three suns ago."

"That was a severe disappointment, I know, to such a young heart," replied the Good One. "A young heart, but a big, brave heart."

"I brought the rice plant six suns before the time of harvest, Father. I—I could not wait, for there was no more food. And, the dipper and I could find no more water." He tucked the rice into the deep pocket.

The Good One rose. "Come with me to the Temple. While I attend to the tea gathering, do you improve your time with counting the rice grains. It is now the time of short shadows. You have until the time of closing of the flowers to complete the count. But first you must eat and bathe."

A servant appeared with a tray on which was a pot of tea and two small cups.

"That is good, Chang. The boy is tired and hungry."

Silently Chang set the tray on the bench and poured the tea, handing one cup to the priest, the other one to Li Lun.

Li Lun sipped and smacked his lips. "It is my first cup of tea in almost four moon changes! Thank you, most gracious Father." He drained the cup in several famished gulps.

"Give to Li Lun water for bathing and clean garments,"

the Keeper of the Temple commanded Chang. "Then give him food. He has had but little food in many days." The priest returned his cup.

Chang did not reply, but he refilled Li Lun's cup before he picked up his poles and bundles and started up the Temple steps.

Li Lun gulped the second cup of tea hungrily. Then he set the cup on the tray, picked up his jacket and, with a bow to the priest, followed Chang.

"When Li Lun has bathed and eaten food," the priest called after Chang, "show him to the sunset room. I will meet him there."

Chang turned at the top of the steps and bowed to the priest.

Li Lun followed Chang down a red-and-black tiled hallway which smelled strongly of sandalwood. At the far end of the hall, Chang laid Li Lun's belongings on an open portico. Then he opened a sliding door and pointed to a red tile pool.

"The water is warm," Chang said as he placed soap and towels at the edge of the pool. "Soon I bring clean garments. Then food on the portico." Chang disappeared noiselessly through the sliding door.

Li Lun was speechless. He had never dreamed that there was on Blue Shark Island such a lovely place for bathing. He removed his dirty, tattered clothing and slipped into the sunken pool. The hot tea had relaxed him and the warm water tempted him to sleep. But he knew that he must not sleep. Too many things were waiting for him. Besides, he was starved, and Chang had said he would soon bring food.

Li Lun hurried through his bath. So quietly did Chang come in with clean clothing that Li Lun did not hear him. But when he was ready for them, a fresh white blouse and blue trousers were there on a bench, waiting for him.

When he was dressed, Li Lun pushed open the door which led to the portico. His poles and bundles were still there, with his jacket on top of them. Near them Chang had set a small black lacquered table and bamboo chair. On the table was a pot of tea.

Li Lun sat down and poured himself a cup of the steaming beverage. It tasted delicious!

As he drank, Chang came in with a tray and placed before him a plate with rice cakes and steamed seaweed.

Li Lun picked up the chopsticks and put some of the rice to his lips. "It is seasoned with shrimp," he breathed. "Ah, but it is good!" He sipped tea noisily between huge gulps of food.

Under a covered dish he found bamboo sprouts. "Bamboo sprouts I have never eaten," he murmured. His lips trembled. Almost the Good One and Chang were too good to him. Tears smarted his eyes as he glanced at the tray of fruit which Chang had set on the table before leaving.

When Li Lun finished his meal, Chang appeared and bowed. "The Father wishes you to come to the sunset room."

He led the way through the hallway down which they had come.

Li Lun felt in the deep pocket of his jacket. Yes, the rice was still there. He followed Chang into a room with black tiled floor and cream-colored tiled walls. As Li Lun's eyes accustomed themselves to the change in colors, he saw several black chairs and two small tables. They stood beside a window which overlooked the sea where white waves splashed high over rocks.

"I can count my grains here," murmured Li Lun.

Chang left the room, and Li Lun was alone.

He pulled the rice plant from his deep pocket and sat on the floor where the rice grains showed against the black tiles. Then he began his counting.

He counted the grains by moon changes, as he had counted the stones on the mountain. The grain heads had separated into three blades. The shortest blade had two grains less than a moon change. The longest blade had a moon change and a half. The third blade had three grains more than a moon change.

When he had finished counting, Li Lun found that he had almost as many grains as he had spent days on the mountain. He had not thought one grain could grow so many kernels!

The hot tea and the well-cooked food made Li Lun drowsy. Tucking the empty grain head into the deep pocket, he folded his jacket and placed it on the floor for a pillow. He laid his head upon it and in an instant was sound asleep.

When Li Lun awoke, he was conscious of droning sounds.

He turned toward the window on the side of the room opposite the sea. He could see that a crowd of people had collected in front of the Temple. Li Lun stood beside the window where he could see them without being seen. He stretched to his tiptoes to look for his most honorable father and his most beautiful mother. But he did not see them. When Teng Lun saw the rice, Li Lun wondered, would he still call his son a coward?

Now the Keeper of the Temple appeared, dressed in his long black robe and with the little round cap on his head.

"Have you counted the grains of rice?" he asked quietly.

Li Lun nodded.

"How many grains were there on the one plant?" the Good One asked, holding out his hand for the rice.

"Enough for three moon changes and for another half moon change," replied Li Lun happily. "Almost one grain for every day I was on Lao Shan."

"Good! Come, we shall tell your people."

The priest walked to the edge of the outer steps where the people were. Li Lun followed him.

Raising his hand, the priest waited for the people to grow quiet. Then he pulled Li Lun gently to his side and placed his hand on the boy's shoulder.

"This boy was called a coward," the Good One spoke. "He was taunted because of his fear of deep sea water. He was sent to the top of Lao Shan to spend four moon changes alone. He was given seven small grains and commanded to grow rice from them —to grow rice on the top of Lao Shan."

A ripple of wonder ran through the crowd.

Li Lun's knees trembled. He shifted from one foot to another, so that the people would not see how he shook.

"He has done what not one of you on this island has done," the priest went on. "He has grown rice. Grown it at the top of Lao Shan. Grown it from the seven grains given to him by his father. Two plants were carried away by gulls. Five plants he has brought back with him. The gulls and rats ate the four which you see in his hands."

Trembling, Li Lun held up the dried stalks.

"This plant—" the priest took the empty rice head from Li Lun and held it up—"this one plant grew ninety-nine grains. The boy was ordered to bring back seven times the number of grains he planted. He has brought back more than double that. During four long moon changes he has struggled and toiled. He had to carry up the mountain the soil in which to plant the rice. He had to drive away the gulls and the rats. He had to carry water to the plants with a small dipper, only to have the sun drink up the water before his eyes. He has toiled harder than the deep-sea fishermen. And now Li Lun has brought his harvest home."

A swell of happy murmurings passed through the crowd. Li Lun's knees knocked each other in their trembling. But the

Keeper of the Temple had not finished his story.

"The wise men of old have said that 'the production of a grain of rice is as great a work as the creation of a mountain,'" he told the people.

"Ah, Li Lun did that!" came hums of approval for the boy who had refused to go on his man-making fishing trip.

"Li Lun has proved that it is possible to grow rice on Blue Shark Island," the priest continued. "No one has done this for many years. Not since the destruction of Mei Shan. . . . We are a fisher people. We have brought our rice from across the sea, over rough and treacherous waters. But now I shall ask Li Lun to teach other boys how to grow rice. Not on Lao Shan, but right here on our Temple grounds. From now on, the Island of the Blue Shark will have both fishermen and growers of rice."

"Ah!" Murmurs of pleased surprise swept the throng.

The priest turned to Li Lun and smiled.

Li Lun bowed low and mumbled, "Thank you, most honorable Keeper of the Temple."

Through the crowd a man and a woman came pushing until finally they stood at the bottom of the steps. Li Lun ran down to greet them.

"My most honorable father! My most beautiful mother!"

"My son!" greeted Wang Lun as she stooped to press her cheek to his. "You have grown the rice!"

Li Lun's father stood looking on coldly. His fellow fisher-

"Li Lun has grown rice."

the Good One tells the people

men watched to see how he would welcome the son who had disobeyed him.

Li Lun held out his hands. "Here, most honorable father, are the plants which the rats and the gulls destroyed. The rice heads are with the Keeper of the Temple."

Teng Lun made no effort to take the broken dried stalks. But his eyes met those of his son with a glint of pride. Wang Lun's hands quickly gathered in the broken stems to cherish.

Li Lun smiled at her gratefully through misty eyes. "And most beautiful mother—" his voice trembled—"here are the dragon bones which you gave me. I did not need them." He drew the small package from his deep pocket and placed it in her hands.

Wang Lun clasped the package tightly. "Li Lun," she whispered, "I am deeply proud of you. You are a lad of courage."